MW00814777

No Snow for Christmas

Published by Picture Window Books
A Capstone Imprint
1710 Roe Crest Drive
North Mankato, Minnesota 56003
www.capstonepub.com

Copyright © 2014 Picture Window Books
All rights reserved. No part of this publication may be reproduced
in whole or in part, or stored in a retrieval system, or transmitted in any form
or by any means, electronic, mechanical, photocopying, recording,
or otherwise, without written permission of the publisher.

Library of Congress Cataloging-in-Publication Data is available
on the Library of Congress website.

ISBN: 978-1-4795-2158-6

Summary: Without any snow in sight and Christmas Eve tomorrow,
Fawn Braun and the villagers of Pfeffernut gather and try to create snow.

Designer:
Russell John Griesmer

Photo Credits:
ShutterStock / Ambient Ideas, cover, backcover
ShutterStock / Attitude, cover, backcover, 1, 2, 3, 32
ShutterStock / Mutation, cover
ShutterStock / Eliks, endsheets

Printed in China.
032013 007228RRDF13

No Snow for Christmas

Written by Jill Kalz

Illustrated by Sahin Erkocak

a capstone imprint www.capstonepub.com

Fawn Braun had never been so worried.

Tomorrow was Christmas Eve, and all of Pfeffernut County lay brown, dull, and dusty. No snow on the streets. No snow on the benches, buses, or trees.

The empty fields stretched wide.

Dry weeds poked from the ditches like old broom bristles.

Would Fawn make a strawman instead of a snowman? Dirt angels instead of snow angels? Would this year's moonlight sleigh ride be a stuffy ride to town in the family car?

"Christmas won't be Christmas without snow!" Fawn cried.

"Now, dear," her mother said, "don't worry. The snow will come when it's ready. Nothing you do will hurry it along. Just be still."

But Fawn wasn't very good at being still.

That night, at the town meeting, Fawn spoke up.

"Everyone," she said, "we have an emergency!
If we don't make some snow tomorrow,
Christmas won't come to Pfeffernut County."

The townspeople gasped.

"Oh, no! What a pickle!" they cried.

"Christmas will pass us by," Fawn continued.
"It will skip north to Hoogledoo Falls.
They always have snow in Hoogledoo Falls.
We won't have any presents or carols or sugar cookies."

The mayor called for a vote. The answer was clear. The townspeople agreed to meet at the Braun farm at four o'clock the next day. They would make snow.

"Think white," Fawn said.
"Think flaky. Think fluffy.
Think floaty and sparkly, too."

Before she went to bed, Fawn took a long look at her family's Christmas tree. The ornaments shimmered. Pfeffernut County would have snow tomorrow. And Christmas would come as planned.

Fawn was sure of it!

The following day, a nervous group of snowmakers gathered at the Braun farm.

Louie was the first to try. He crushed chalk in his big hands and blew it into the air. He tried flour and powdered sugar, too.

"It's white," Fawn said. "But it doesn't have much shape. It just looks like **dust**."

Next came Farmer Cap. The strange old man shook bags of popcorn into the air.

"It has the right shape," Fawn said.
"But it isn't **soft** and **fluffy**."

The other farmers tossed cotton balls
and mini marshmallows into the air.

"It's soft and fluffy," Fawn said.
"But it isn't **floaty** or **sparkly**."

Finally, Liza Dietz blew bubbles into the air.

"It's floaty and sparkly," Fawn said.
"But it isn't cold. Oh, this just won't do!"

Fawn's mother was right. No one could hurry the snow along, not even the good-hearted folks of Pfeffernut County. Fawn knew she had to break the sad news: no snow, no Christmas.

But before she could speak, something **magical** happened.
Everyone was laughing and singing.
They were tumbling and twirling.
They were sharing and toasting.
Their cheer lit up the county from end to end.

Fawn smiled. It was the merriest
Christmas she had ever seen!

No snow fell in Pfeffernut County on Christmas.
None fell on New Year's Day, either.
The snow came when it was ready,
and not a moment sooner.

And Fawn Braun was just fine with that.

The End